HOT-AIR HENRY

by Mary Calhoun * illustrated by Erick Ingraham

MULBERRY BOOKS • New York

Text copyright © 1981 by Mary Calhoun
Illustrations copyright © 1981 by Erick Ingraham

Inquiries should be addressed to
William Morrow and Company, Inc.,
1350 Avenue of the Americas, New York, NY 10019.

Printed in the United States of America.
15   14   13   12   11   10   9   8   7   6
First Mulberry edition, 1986

Library of Congress Cataloging in Publication Data

Calhoun, Mary   Hot-air Henry.
    Summary: A sassy Siamese cat stows away on a hot-air balloon
and ends up taking a fur-raising flight across the mountains.
    [1. Cats—Fiction. 2. Hot-air ballons—Fiction]
I. Ingraham, Erick. II. Title.
PZ7.C1278Hrm   [E]   80-26189   ISBN 0-688-04068-3 (pbk.)

To Hot-Air Michael
with heart-felt thanks

Henry wanted to fly.
Everybody in his family
had gone up with the balloon,
but The Man always declared,
"I'm not flying with that cat!"

The Man had been taking pilot's lessons,
and this time he was going to solo.
Henry grumbled and his tail switched,
as he watched the people crunch around
on the crusty March snow.

The Kid and The Woman held open the mouth
of the colorful balloon,
while The Man blew it up
with a gasoline-powered fan.
Then the Instructor blasted
warm air into the balloon
from the burner mounted on a frame below it.
"Watch your fuel gauge," he told The Man.
"You don't want those propane tanks to run dry.
And stay away from those power lines
on Colson Hill."

At last the beautiful balloon
stood fat in the air.
The Woman and The Instructor loaded
the fan into the truck.
The Kid held down the basket
while The Man jumped out to get his camera,
which he'd forgotten.

Henry saw his chance to stow away.
He raced across the snow
and leaped up to the basket.

One of his claws snagged on the cord
that fired the burner,
and there was a horrible roar.
"Grab that cat!" yelled The Man.
The Kid lunged for Henry and slipped on the snow.
The burner kept roaring.

Flames heated the air, and up rose the balloon.
Up rose Henry, up, up, and away!
Henry was flying!

He shook his claw loose from the cord,
and the burner stopped roaring,
but the balloon kept on lifting.
Henry crouched on the leather rim of the basket,
digging in his claws.
Below the ground fell away,
and the people shouted and waved.
Yet the basket didn't feel as if it were moving,
and Henry wasn't afraid.

"Yow-meowl!" he called down to The Kid.
He was Hot-Air Henry, the flying cat!

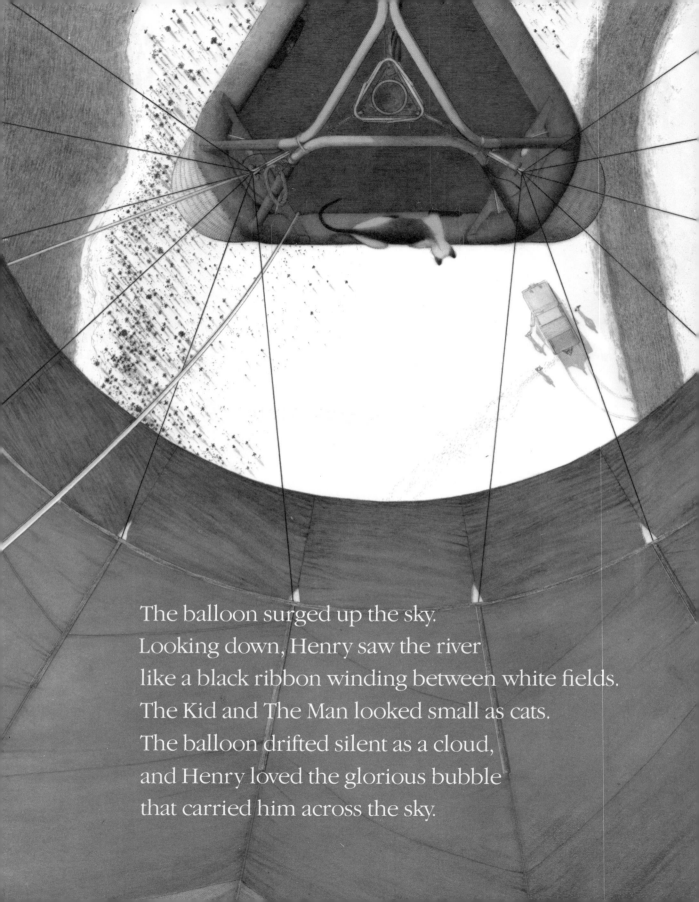

The balloon surged up the sky.
Looking down, Henry saw the river
like a black ribbon winding between white fields.
The Kid and The Man looked small as cats.
The balloon drifted silent as a cloud,
and Henry loved the glorious bubble
that carried him across the sky.

Balanced against a post on the rim of the basket,
Henry floated above his snowy world.
To a tune of The Kid's about
"Sailing, sailing, over the bounding main,"
Henry sang, "Yow-me Ow-me Ow-meow-meow."
He was the cat to sail the skies!

But now he'd had his flight,
and it was The Man's turn to solo.
Time to go down. How?
Henry stood up and tried pulling the cord.
The whooshing roar of the burner scared him,
and he tottered on the edge of the basket.
To keep from falling, he clung to the cord,
and the burner kept roaring
and the balloon rose higher.
That was not the way to get down out of the sky.

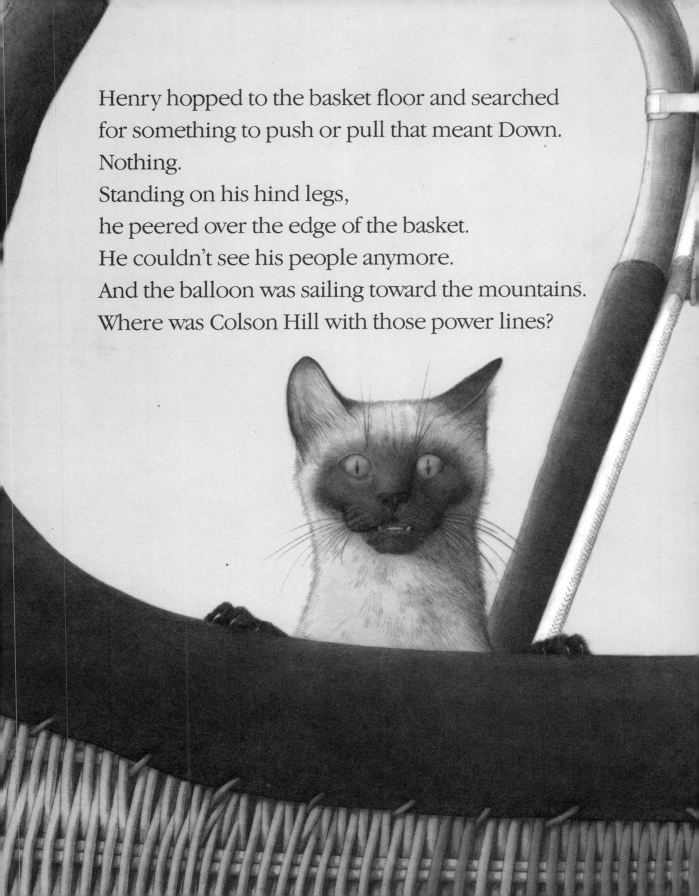

Henry hopped to the basket floor and searched
for something to push or pull that meant Down.
Nothing.
Standing on his hind legs,
he peered over the edge of the basket.
He couldn't see his people anymore.
And the balloon was sailing toward the mountains.
Where was Colson Hill with those power lines?

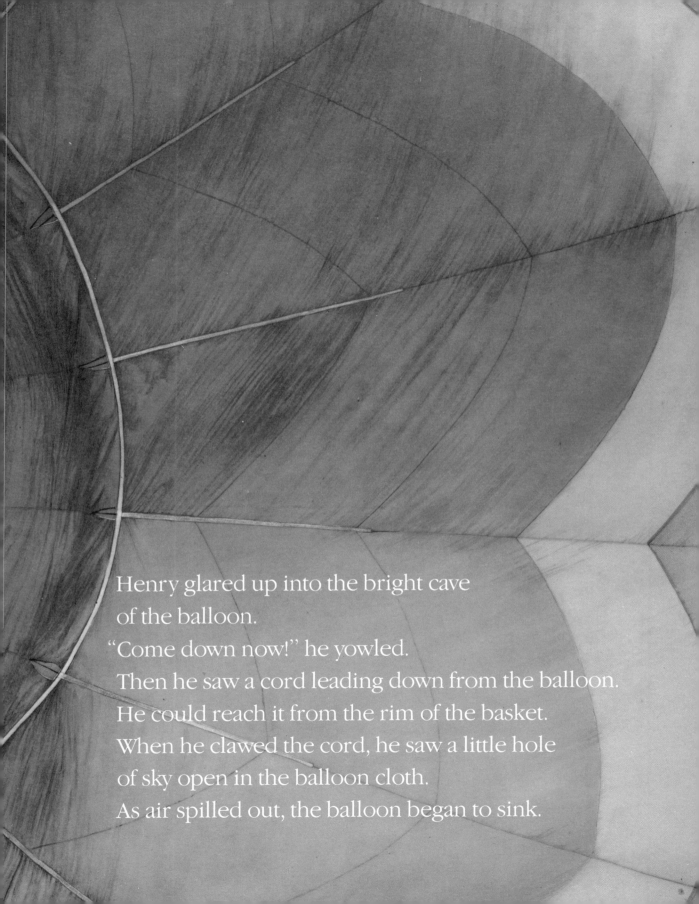

Henry glared up into the bright cave
of the balloon.
"Come down now!" he yowled.
Then he saw a cord leading down from the balloon.
He could reach it from the rim of the basket.
When he clawed the cord, he saw a little hole
of sky open in the balloon cloth.
As air spilled out, the balloon began to sink.

Faster and faster, the basket dropped,
toward the ground—too fast!
Henry let go of the cord.
More slowly the basket sank toward the river,
black rushing water—a splash down?

No, the basket crunched on the snowy bank.
"Ha!" breathed Henry.
But the basket bounced up in the air again,
touch and bounce, over the snow.
"Stop it!" Henry yelled at the balloon.
"I'm not a yo-yo!"

Ahead were some willows dotted with blackbirds
singing, "O-kal-lee!"
The basket bounded over the tops of the trees,
brushing out birds.
"Tchk, tchk!"
The redwings swarmed around the basket.
Henry snatched at this bird, that bird.
Missed! Missed!

The birds whisked upward, teasing,
"O-kal-lee, you can't catch me!"
Henry forgot about landing.
"I can too!" he yowled.
Standing on the rim, he pulled the burner cord.
Roar, the basket zoomed after the birds.
"Yow-meow!" Henry chased blackbirds up the sky.

But the balloon overshot the birds,
and they settled back down in the willows.
The balloon sailed on toward the mountains.
The wrong direction,
away from The Man and The Kid.
"Go back!" yowled Henry at the beautiful bubble.
But the balloon went where the wind took it.

Below a lazy eagle coasted on an air current
flowing in the right direction.
Maybe if the balloon dropped just to that level—

Henry crept around the rim of the basket
and pulled the air-spilling cord.
Slowly the balloon sank and began to come around.
It didn't take off after the eagle
like the tail of a kite,
but it was going more toward The Kid than away.
"Yow-meow-ee!" Henry sang out.
He'd show that balloon who was boss!
He, Hot-Air Henry, would bring the balloon
right back where it started from.

He toed his way along the rim
and pulled the burner cord just a flick
to keep the balloon from dropping too low too soon.
At the roar of the burner,
the eagle flapped up in surprise.
"What in the sky!" screeched the eagle.

The big bird circled the fat contraption.
Henry watched anxiously.
That eagle better not peck a hole in his balloon!
"Snaa!" Henry hissed.
"Scat! Get away from there!"

He made the burner roar.

"Help!" squalled the eagle.

"What a cat, to roar like that!"

The eagle winged away from the fearsome feline.

Henry spared a paw to smooth his whiskers.
Then he peered down, narrowing his blue eyes
at the brightness of the snow.
Below on a road was a truck,
and The Kid's head stuck out the window.
The chase truck was following the balloon.
"Yow-yow, right now!" sang Henry.

He got over to the rip cord, spilled air,
and the balloon dropped.
Just then, "Honk, honk,"
came a squadron of geese flying straight at him.
"Honk," called the geese, "honk, honk!"
What did they mean, *honk*?
He would *not* get out of the way!

The V of geese broke up around the balloon,
and they rushed up and down, squawking.
But the head goose sat down
on the edge of the basket by the burner cord.
"Snaaa!" hissed Henry.
"Get out of my basket! You can't perch there!"
"Honk! I can too,"
said the head goose, perching there.
The balloon kept sinking.

"Hey, cat!"
The Kid's shout made Henry look.
The basket was headed
for some high-strung power lines.
At last he'd found Colson Hill.
He had to fire the burner to lift quickly,
or he'd sizzle on the wires.
But the goose guarded the burner cord.

Henry started toward the goose, "Snaaa!"
"Hiss!" answered the goose, hunching its wings.
Henry had never fought a goose,
and he didn't like to try for the first time
while balancing like a tightrope walker.
But he had to fire the burner!

Henry sprang.
Over the goose's head he leaped,
onto the goose's back, and clawed at the cord.
As Henry flew over,
a sharp nip of a beak on his tail made him yowl.

But when the burner boomed,
the goose jumped into the air.
And Henry fell off its back—into the basket,
which soared up over the power lines.
Henry licked his throbbing tail,
while the geese regrouped and flew on. "Honk, honk."

Then Henry pulled the rip cord
to bring the basket down.
The Kid and The Man jumped out of the truck.
The basket bounced once over the snow toward them,
as Henry hung on to the air-spilling cord.
The Man grabbed the dragline, then the basket.

"Mew." Henry drooped against a post.
The Man might be mad at him
for going off with the balloon.
Henry leaned his head on The Man's chest.
"Purr-mew!" he begged pardon
for soloing sooner than The Man.

"Wow, some high-flying cat!" said The Kid,
    punching down balloon cloth.
"Purr-mew!" said Henry, smoothing The Man's chest.
  Wise old flying cat.